A GIANT Problem!

by Richard Fowler

BARRON'S
New York · Toronto

Early one morning, about a hundred years ago,
in a little village deep in the country,
a boy was awakened from his sleep by a crow
tapping on his bedroom window.
Tap-tap, tap-tap!

"Follow me," said the crow, "and I will
let you in on a secret!"

The boy followed the crow into the forest
that surrounded the village.
After a long walk, the crow led the boy to
a tall tree that stood alone in a small clearing.

"Climb up!" said the crow.

The boy climbed up through the branches,
until at last he came to the top of the tree.

In front of him stood the strangest building
he had ever seen!

"Go on, take a look inside," cackled the crow.

"I will," said the boy timidly.

He climbed up to the top window on one side of the building.

At first the shutters wouldn't open, but the boy wouldn't give up. He hung on with both hands and pulled with all his might.

All at once, the shutters flew apart, and he found he was staring into a huge blue eye that was staring back at him!

He opened the shutters on the other side
and found another huge blue eye!
When he opened the shutters of the lower window,
he discovered an enormous mouth!

"HELLO," said the mouth. "It's good to see you!"

"Er, um, hello," said the boy. "Who are you?"

"I'm a giant," said the mouth.

"What are you doing here?" asked the boy.

"I was tricked by a woodcutter," said the giant,
"a hundred years ago!"

"What happened?" asked the boy.

"You get me out and I'll tell you," said the giant.

"I'll have to get some help," said the boy.

"Well please hurry," said the giant.
"My legs ache!"

The boy hurried back to the village
and told everyone about the building with the
giant trapped inside . . . They all laughed!

"Don't be silly," they said. "There's no such
thing as a giant! Whatever will you think of next?"

Later the same day, there was a terrible storm.
The wind blew so hard that the walls of the houses
caved in, and the roofs were tossed high in the air!
The rain washed away the land,
and the village was completely destroyed.

The next morning the villagers came out of
the forest where they had taken shelter from
the storm.

"What are we going to do?" they asked each other.
"There's nothing left!"

The boy was sitting on a plank of wood where
his house used to be when he saw the crow.

"You may laugh," said the boy, "but I bet the only building left standing is the giant's house! We could use the wood and materials from that to rebuild the entire village."

"What are we waiting for?" cried the villagers.

"Come on," and they set off after the boy.

They crashed through the forest and climbed up through the trees, and there, undamaged by the storm, stood the strange building with the giant peering out! An eerie silence fell over them. Finally someone said:

"There really *is* a giant. The boy was right!"

"He seems like a friendly giant," said the boy, "and we do need the wood."

"Come on," said the blacksmith. "Let's get started!" With a cheer, the villagers set about dismantling the building.

"HOORAY!" boomed the giant. "I'll soon be able to stretch my legs!"

The villagers removed the roof and the upper
parts of the building. Gradually, the giant was able to
move his arms and legs and helped to take off
the larger pieces.

Suddenly the giant yelled: "STOP!
I can do the rest myself."

The villagers got out of the way just in time.
The giant burst out of the building, jumped in the air,
punched a cloud, and then turned cartwheels
across the countryside!

After an hour or two the giant calmed down and carefully tiptoed over the trees to the clearing where the village once stood.

He was so pleased to be free once more that he offered to help rebuild the houses.

Within a week the village had been completely rebuilt.

Everyone was very happy, and said how useful it was to have their own friendly giant.

Then the problems began!

Farmers complained when their crops and wheat fields were flattened by the giant's feet!

The giant ate so much food the village store was empty, and so were the villagers' stomachs!

When the giant sneezed, all the washing on the clothes lines was blown away, or landed in the dirt and had to be washed all over again!

When the giant took a bath in the river everyone took a bath! Because the river overflowed and flooded all the houses!

But worst of all . . .

. . . when the giant slept, he snored!
Giant snores that went
AAAAUUUUHHHHFFFF. . . .WHEEEEOOOOOHHHH!
They kept the whole village awake and shook
the walls and foundations of the houses.

On one of these nights the villagers gathered
together to discuss their giant problem.
Even the boy agreed, the village would be destroyed
again if they didn't do something soon.
Sadly they decided the giant would have to go.

The next morning they asked the giant if he would mind sleeping further away from the village, in an old unused quarry.

The giant agreed. Late that night, when the giant was sound asleep, the villagers felled the tallest trees in the forest. Working very quietly, they laid the trees across the quarry from one side to the other.

Then they covered the trees with tons of earth
and rock. They built a well above the giant's head
to make sure he could breathe
and then went home for some well-earned sleep!
The villagers soon forgot about the giant, and
he never bothered them again.

Early one morning a hundred years later,
an old black crow circled over a field.
The crow dropped out of the sky and landed on a tent.
The two children asleep in the tent were awakened
by the sound of the crow scratching on the canvas.
Scratch, scratch, scratch, scratch.

"Follow me," said the crow, "and I will let
you in on a secret!"

The children followed the crow up a hill.
At the top of the hill hidden in some trees,
they found a well . . .

"Shout down the well," said the crow.
The children yelled down the well. They shouted:
"Hello, helloo!"
"HELLO!" a deep voice boomed back.
The children jumped in surprise,
then they peeked over the edge of the well
and saw a huge blue eye staring up at them!
"It must be a giant," they cried.
"What's a giant doing down a well?"

"I'll tell you," said the giant, "as soon as you get me out of here!"

"We'll have to get some help," they replied.

"Hurry up please," said the giant, "my back aches!"
The boy and girl ran down the hill to
tell their parents.

"Wake up Dad, wake up Mom," they shouted.

"There's a giant at the bottom of the well,
and he wants to get out. Please help!"
Their mom and dad just laughed.

"Don't be silly," they said.

"A giant! whatever will you think of next?"